Disney PRINCESS
MULAN

Disney

H hachette

Long ago, the Emperor of China had a great
wall built to keep out his enemies, the Huns.
In those days, a son honoured his family by
showing bravery as a soldier. A daughter's duty
was to be a good wife.

When a girl was ready to get married, the local Matchmaker would look for a suitable husband for her. A visit to the Matchmaker could be very nerve-wracking!

One day, a young girl called Mulan was getting
ready to visit the Matchmaker. She was nervous.
What would the Matchmaker think of her?

Mulan's mother fixed a pretty comb in Mulan's
hair, while her grandmother hung something on
her belt. It was a cricket in a tiny cage, to bring
her granddaughter luck.

But at the Matchmaker's, everything went wrong.
The cricket escaped and caused mayhem. When the
Matchmaker's robe caught fire, Mulan put the fire
out by pouring a teapot of water over her!

"You'll never bring honour on your family!"
shrieked the furious Matchmaker.

Mulan's father, Fa Zhou, tried to cheer his daughter up. He was sure that one day, Mulan would make her family very proud.

Just then,
a drumbeat
announced
the arrival
of Chi Fu, the
Emperor's advisor.
"The Huns have
invaded China!" he announced.
"By order of the Emperor, one man from
every family must serve in the Imperial Army."

Mulan knew that her father was no longer able to fight, so she decided she would take his place by pretending to be a boy. She took his army papers, then cut off her hair with his sword.

Dressed in her father's old uniform, Mulan
mounted his horse and rode off into the night.

When her parents realised what Mulan had done,
they were very worried. Impersonating a soldier was
a crime punishable by death!

When Mulan's grandmother prayed for her, the
Ancestors decided to send a Guardian to protect the
girl. A little dragon called Mushu volunteered, but
the Ancestors weren't sure he was up to the job, so
they set him a test.

Mushu's test was to use his gong to awaken the most powerful Guardian of all. But Mushu banged the gong so hard that the statue cracked and crumbled to pieces!

"Oh man, they're gonna kill me!" wailed Mushu.

Cri-Kee, Mulan's cricket, gave Mushu some advice. Maybe if he helped the girl to become a hero, the Ancestors would forgive him and let him be a Guardian again. The pair explained their plan to a surprised Mulan.

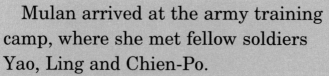

Mulan arrived at the army training
camp, where she met fellow soldiers
Yao, Ling and Chien-Po.

Captain Shang, the trainer,
worked the recruits very hard, but
Mulan showed such determination
that Shang and the other soldiers
were impressed.

Finally, the trainees were
ready. It was time to go to war.

A few days later, the Huns, led by Shan-Yu, attacked Mulan's unit. Shang ordered Mulan to fire the cannons at the enemy. But Mulan disobeyed. Instead, she fired a cannonball into the snowy mountainside and caused an avalanche!

Shan-Yu attacked Mulan, but it was too late – he and his troops were soon buried in the snow.

Mulan was a hero. She had saved the army and beaten the Huns.

"I owe you my life," said Shang.

But before she could reply Mulan, who had been wounded in the battle, collapsed to the ground.

At the hospital, a doctor found out that Mulan
was really a girl. Shang was stunned by the news.
  "I only did it to save my father," explained
Mulan. But Shang knew that Mulan would have to
be punished.

Shang raised his sword, but couldn't bring himself to hurt the girl who had saved his life. He rode off, leaving Mulan on the frozen mountain.

Just then, Mulan spotted Shan-Yu and five of his men entering the Imperial City.

Mulan caught up with Shang, who was riding
through the city in a victory parade.
"Shang!" she called. "The Huns are here in the city!"
"Why should I believe you?" replied Shang coldly.

The Huns forced their way into the palace and seized the Emperor. But Mulan and her soldier friends slipped into the palace dressed as women and managed to overpower the Huns.

Shan-Yu was about to attack the Emperor, but Shang appeared and disarmed him just in time!

The Emperor was carried to safety by Chien-Po, one of the soldiers.

Shan-Yu escaped and set off to find Mulan.
"Ready, Mushu?" asked Mulan as Shan-Yu
approached.

Quick as a flash, the little dragon launched a
rocket towards Shan-Yu. He was gone forever!

As a thank-you, the Emperor presented Mulan
with his own pendant and Shan-Yu's sword.

"The world will know that you saved China!" he
declared. And then he bowed to Mulan as a sign of
his respect for her.

When Mulan returned home, her whole family were thrilled to see her.

Soon afterwards, Mulan had a surprise visit from Shang – and her proud parents could tell at once that the couple were falling deeply in love.

As for Mushu, he got his wish too – the Ancestors made him an official Guardian again!